Stephanie Smith

WALT DISNEY PRODUCTIONS
presents

SINDBAD the Sailor

Random House
New York

Book Club Edition

First American Edition

Copyright © 1978 by Walt Disney Productions.
All rights reserved under International and Pan-American
Copyright Conventions. Published in the United States by
Random House, Inc., New York, and simultaneously in Canada
by Random House of Canada Limited, Toronto. Originally
published in Denmark as SINDBAD SOFAREREN by Gutenberghus
Bladene, Copenhagen.
ISBN: 0-394-84118-2   ISBN: 0-394-94118-7 (lib. bdg.)

Manufactured in the United States of America
890   ABCDEFGHIJK

It was a rainy day.

Huey, Louie, and Dewey were sad,
because they could not go out and play.

"Don't be sad," said Grandma Duck.
"I know what we can do."

She went over to the bookcase
and took a red book off the shelf.
"I will read a story to you
about a brave boy named Sindbad."

Grandma Duck sat down
in the big, green chair.

Huey, Louie, and Dewey sat
on the floor in front of her.

Then Grandma Duck began
to read the story.

It went like this:

Once there was a poor boy named Sindbad.
He thought he could get rich by working
as a sailor.
So he took his few things and went
to find a job on a ship.

Sindbad was lucky.

He got a job as a sailor and added
his name to a list
of crew members.

Sindbad's ship set sail.
But soon there was a terrible storm at sea.

The ship was almost
lost in the rain and high waves.
    When the storm was over, all Sindbad
wanted was to be back on land.

At last the ship's crew sighted land.
It was a small island.

Sindbad and four other sailors
headed for shore in a rowboat.

"Maybe I will find riches here,"
thought Sindbad, as they stepped
onto the island.

Sindbad and the other sailors were cold,
so they built a fire to warm themselves.

But just then the ground
began to shake.
And they were thrown high
into the air.

The island was really a giant whale
that had been sleeping!
The hot fire had awakened him.
He quickly dove to the bottom of the ocean.
And the sailors were thrown into the water.

Sindbad sank down, down, down into the ocean.
He was sure that he would drown.

When Sindbad came up again,
he could not see the ship.

But luckily a barrel
floated past him,
and he got inside.

He used his shirt for a sail.
And the wind carried him to
a beautiful island.

"Maybe I will find riches
here," said Sindbad
as he walked
on shore.

He saw fruit trees, birds, and flowers.
But there were no houses or people.

Suddenly Sindbad saw a large, white shape
in the distance.

"Maybe it is a house," he said to himself.
"I will go see."

When he got closer, he saw
that it was a huge egg.
He had never before seen anything
like it!

While Sindbad was looking at the egg,
a giant bird flew out of the sky.

Spreading its wings wide,
the bird landed near Sindbad.

Sindbad quickly tied himself
to the bird's foot.
"Maybe this bird will fly
to a big city," thought Sindbad.

The huge bird took off again.
Sindbad held tight to the bird's foot
as they flew into the air over a large city.
When Sindbad looked down and saw
how high they were, he was so afraid.

But finally the bird landed gently
on the ground.

Sindbad carefully untied himself.

Then he ran as fast and as far away
as he could.

The next morning he came to a castle
with a big, wooden door.

"What will I find behind that door?"
thought Sindbad.

He went inside and found some bones
on the floor.

"I wonder what these big bones are,"
said Sindbad.

"Maybe a giant lives here."

"Right you are," said a loud voice.
Turning around, Sindbad found he was standing
beside a giant.

The giant grabbed Sindbad
in his huge hand.

Sindbad was ready
to fight for his life.

But then the giant said, "You are too small
to eat. There is not enough meat on you."

He put Sindbad back
down on the floor.

Sindbad ran away as fast
as he could.

The next day Sindbad
came to a beautiful city.
There was a fountain in
the middle of the square.

Sindbad sat down on the fountain to rest.

"Maybe I will get rich
in this city,"
he thought.

Sindbad asked a friendly man how he could
get rich in that city.

"The Sultan loves coconuts," the man said.
"He will give a prize to anyone who brings him some."

"That sounds easy," said Sindbad.

"It isn't," said the man, "because the coconuts
are guarded by a giant."

But Sindbad decided to try.
He set out for the coconut grove.
And luck was with him!
Four monkeys were playing
in a coconut tree, but the
giant was nowhere to be seen.

The monkeys thought that Sindbad
wanted to play catch with them.

They grabbed coconuts out of the trees
and threw them at Sindbad.

Sindbad quickly filled his sack full.

Sindbad hurried back to the city.

Just as he got there, the Sultan
passed by.

The Sultan was riding a large elephant,
and his servants were walking alongside.

"If you please, Sultan," called Sindbad,
"I have some coconuts for you."

The Sultan stopped and leaned over.

"You say you have coconuts?" he asked. "How did you get them?"

Sindbad told his story to the Sultan.

"You were very brave to go to the giant's grove and bring me these coconuts," said the Sultan. "You shall be rewarded."

The Sultan gave Sindbad gold and jewels.

"Hooray! I'm rich!" shouted Sindbad.

Sindbad decided to sail back to his own land.
The friendly man came to wave good-by.
Sindbad waved back.

He was very happy.

The Sultan's gold and jewels had made him
a rich man at last.

"So Sindbad returned home and lived
in comfort for the rest of his life,"
said Grandma Duck as she closed the book
and stood up.

"What a lucky fellow," said Huey, Louie, and Dewey.

"Yes, but don't forget that he was also brave and clever!" said Grandma Duck.